CHALLENGING TECHNOPOLY

THE VISION
OF
JOHN HENRY

ALI RASHID ABDULLAH

Illustrated by Avery Liell-Kok

AuthorHouse™ LLC
1663 Liberty Drive
Bloomington, IN 47403
www.authorhouse.com
Phone: 1-800-839-8640

Published by AuthorHouse 04/28/2014

ISBN: 978-1-4918-6651-1 (sc)
978-1-4918-6652-8 (e)

Library of Congress Control Number: 2014903224

Any people depicted in stock imagery provided by Thinkstock are models,
and such images are being used for illustrative purposes only.
Certain stock imagery © Thinkstock.

This book is printed on acid-free paper.

authorHOUSE®

To Durriyya

Your faith and encouragement have been my sustenance.

Acknowledgements

<u>Challenging Technopoly: The Vision of John Henry</u> is an excerpt from a manuscript I am currently in the process of concluding. The subject is the evolving identity of the Black/African American ex-slave people of the United States of America. In the course of these writings, I have come to see John Henry as a pivotal character in this evolution.

I must note that during this heyday of technological adaptation, my perspective is not always well-received, to say the least. Consequently, I want to express my gratitude to the following individuals who have been a source of assistance and encouragement in this project.

I'll begin by thanking my daughters Rahil Abdullah-Lewis and Salima Abdullah-Kleiber; my friends and associates Ali Abdur-Rashid, Hassan Idris Abdur-Rahman, Jim Phillips, Majeedah Shabazz, and Kweli Tutashinda for their efforts and assistance.

I am especially indebted to author Scott Reynolds Nelson for his revealing work on John Henry entitled <u>Steel Drivin' Man</u>. I found both confirmation and inspiration in this wonderfully-researched piece.

By far, however, my greatest appreciation goes to that generation who, in their wisdom and foresight, created The Legend of John Henry. Hopefully, we will recognize their clarity of thought and depth of understanding and avail ourselves of this guidance they have preserved for us.

Table of Contents

Preface

Quiet as it's kept, <u>The Legend of John Henry</u> addresses what many have long considered to be the two most fundamental issues facing African Americans--identity and agenda. Starting with identity, it's no coincidence that "John" and "Henry" were the two most popular names selected by African Americans upon their emancipation from American chattel slavery. The use of these two names is a signal to the audience that this story is about African Americans in the aggregate. Consequently the qualities, attributes, and spirit manifested in the figure of John Henry are a key to the character of the people who emerged from America's womb of bondage with their strength, creativity, and spirituality intact. Which is not to say they did not suffer major casualties during slavery nor ongoing post-traumatic repercussions that continue to this present day. Still, they have met the challenge of embracing and celebrating their blackness. In addition, they have met the challenge of embracing and celebrating their African ancestry. The final step in the evolution of their identity is to realize their essence as a <u>unique</u> people with a unique culture, a unique name, and a unique mission.

It is through John Henry's realization of his identity that he realizes his mission and agenda. As he puts it, he is a "natural man," "more than a machine." But he has found himself in a world where technological innovation is willingly gained at the expense of human welfare. When faced with the relentless encroachment of modern Western technology, John Henry understands his agenda as a natural man is to take a position in opposition to this burgeoning threat to creation. Furthermore, John Henry makes the ultimate sacrifice to forestall the impending destruction in store for his fellow man if they continue this heedless, out-of-control, technological folly.

African Americans have come to respect what is often referred to as "the wisdom of the ancestors" and to seek knowledge and inspiration from the ancient civilizations of Africa. In Challenging Technopoly: The Vision of John Henry, it is being suggested that African Americans more recent ancestors have left wisdom as well--wisdom that deserves their attention and respect.

The Legend of John Henry

It started out the same as any other night when the moon is full. I mean things seemed to be a little off kilter but still within bounds. The Henrys' cat, for example, came and curled up on Mrs. Henry's lap. Now that was a little strange because that cat usually kept as far away from Mrs. Henry as possible. The only interaction they ever had was when there was no one home to feed him, and he would worry her sick rubbing up against her legs and meowing until she got the message.

"You avoid me like poison ivy 'til your belly's empty, don't you," she would remind him.

But it wouldn't shame him. As soon as his belly was full, he wouldn't come near her until the next time no one else was available.

Around midnight, the moon began to get markedly brighter and even brighter still. Golden halos formed around each star. Bats and owls out on their nightly prowls became totally confused when a few hours later roosters began to crow and sparrows began to chirp. But Mr. and Mrs. Henry continued to sleep as peacefully as ever. Meanwhile, little by little, the forest animals had come to the clearing where the Henrys' cabin stood.

When Mr. Henry awoke, there was so much light in the cabin, he thought he had overslept. But just then the big grandfather clock in the front room signaled it was five o'clock in the morning.

Mr. Henry went to the window, pulled aside the curtain, and discovered forest animals of every description gathered in a quiet circle around his cabin. There were foxes sitting next to rabbits. There were deer standing next to wolves. There were snakes lying next to mice.

"What in the world," Mr. Henry murmured to no one in particular.

He turned to tell his wife what he had seen, and the sight he saw there was even more unbelievable. Sitting next to the still-sleeping Mrs. Henry was the biggest newborn baby Mr. Henry had ever seen. That's right...sitting. And in the baby's hand was a little golden hammer about the size of a toothbrush.

"Well who are you," asked Mr. Henry, not really expecting an answer.

"My name is John," was the reply.

And that was just the beginning. Everything young John Henry did was extraordinary. In a week he had a mouthful of teeth and was using them to chew everything in sight. In a month, he was not only walking, he was running.

By the time he was a year old, young John Henry could write his name and read every label on a can or box of food. By then, Mr. Henry had had to clear another acre of farmland just to provide enough food to satisfy the youngster's appetite.

When he was seven, Mrs. Henry had to shop for John Henry's clothes in the men's section. Although, John Henry mostly wore overalls, because he was always working in that garden which took up three acres by then. When John Henry wasn't at work in his father's garden, Mr. Henry hired him out to work in the neighbors' gardens in return for a share of their crops. Feeding John Henry had become a serious concern for his parents.

But John Henry didn't mind the work at all. He would plow the farmers' fields with his bare hands because he loved grasping big handfuls of earth and letting it run through his fingers. That was when everyone started to call John Henry a "natural" man.

The only thing John Henry loved more than plowing was hammering. If there was any kind of hammering work to be done, everyone in the community knew to call on John Henry. By the time he was twelve, John Henry had collected every kind of hammer he could lay his hands on. And the little golden hammer he had in his hand at birth, he wore on a chain around his neck.

Yes sir, John Henry loved to hammer. So by the time the Chesapeake and Ohio Railroad Company started laying track through his town, no one was happier than John Henry. When he took hold of one of those steel drivin' hammers, John Henry felt he had taken his life in his own hands.

From that day on, John Henry was a steel drivin' man for the railroads. He traveled America from side to side and top to bottom. Wherever track was being laid, John Henry would go.

He soon developed the knack of driving steel with a hammer in each hand and was sought after by every railroad company in the country.

He soon developed the knack of driving steel with a hammer in each hand and was sought after by every railroad company in the country. It wasn't only the amount of work John Henry did that made him so popular. It was his spirit. When John Henry started swinging his hammers, his spirit would energize the entire crew. His clear deep bass voice would sing out, accented by the rhythmic ringing of his hammers driving spikes of steel.

Drivin' steel is what I do...pinggg, pinggg

Layin' railroad track with my crew...pinggg, pinggg

Hammers ringin' through the land...clanggg, clanggg

Makin' music like a band...clanggg, clanggg

So when you hear John's song...binggg, binggg

You'll always want to sing along...binggg, binggg

Well, one day John Henry was laying track in West Virginia. The crew was camped near the entrance to Big Bend Tunnel. The next day's plan was to finish boring the final stretch through the tunnel.

Earlier that day, a dealer from up North had brought a new machine called a steam drill into camp. He had said his steam drill could do the work of ten men, and he had come to demonstrate just how powerful it was.

That evening around the campfire everyone was fascinated with the steam drill. It was rumored that the company was planning to buy a number of these machines, and most of the men worried about their jobs. John Henry was a little worried himself, but it wasn't about his job. What was worrying John

Henry was a thought that had been nagging at him ever since he had heard about the machine and what the dealer said it would do.

"A machine can never replace a man," thought John Henry. "A man is more than a machine." And now that he was face-to-face with the steam drill, that thought was nagging him worse than ever.

"A machine can never replace a man," thought John Henry. "A man is more than a machine." And now that he was face-to-face with the steam drill, that thought was nagging him worse than ever. All of a sudden, the words erupted out of John Henry like hot lava from a volcano.

"I can beat that machine."

Everyone stopped speaking. The thick silence filled the empty space between the men. Meanwhile, a scornful grin had etched its way across the face of the Northern dealer.

"Who wants to put his money where John Henry just put his mouth?" he sneered.

The men looked at John Henry and then at the steam drill. The steam drill was a fearsome sight. Its steel-encased body surrounded the engine with the stillness of a coffin. Four slithering hoses protruded from one end like huge venomous snakes. While at the other end, a smokestack squatted at the top like the blunted horn of an angry rhinoceros.

Then the men looked back at John Henry. He towered two feet over the tallest man. The muscles in his arms, legs, and chest were at rest for the moment, but they had all seen the coordinated power of those muscles when John Henry swung his hammers. But against the machine...?

Then the men's eyes fell on John Henry's face. There they beheld a quiet smile of unwavering assurance. His eyes were as tranquil as two pools of motionless water. Peering deeply within their clear depths, the men could see the determination in John Henry's soul.

Released from the grip of John Henry's gaze, one-by-one the men bet whatever money they had on John Henry. The match was set to begin at daybreak, and everyone retired to their respective tents.

The next morning when the men emerged from their tents, John Henry stood waiting at the mouth of Big Bend Tunnel. During the night, their sleep had been briefly interrupted by strong winds that had gotten them off their cots in fear of disaster. But the winds had subsided almost as soon as the men had run out of their tents, so they had all gratefully stumbled back to bed. One of the men had said he saw something in the sky, but whatever it might have been was forgotten in the excitement of the ensuing match.

The crew pulled the steam drill up the slight incline to the tunnel entrance. They had been working for a month burrowing through the rocky core of the mountain and had about 200 more yards to punch through to daylight on the other side.

The steam drill was wheeled into the tunnel on one set of tracks while John Henry advanced up to the wall of rock on the other set of tracks about twenty feet away. It was declared that the first one to cut through to daylight would be the winner.

"Crank 'er up!" shouted the Northerner.

The steam drill coughed a few times and then began to sputter and rumble as its engine started up. John Henry stood silently waiting, his muscles tensed, a slight smile of confidence on his face.

"Ready! Set! Go!" yelled the foreman.

The screeching sound of the steam drill as its bit began to cut into the rock backed the men up several yards. The acrid smell of its burning fuel singed the hair in their nostrils. The smoke from its exhaust made their eyes tear. And the grit that filled the air cut into their skin.

Meanwhile, John Henry had begun to swing his hammers with a slow and steady rhythm-Pinggg! Panggg! Clinggg! Clanggg! The steam drill had gotten out in front to be sure, its screeching bit making the rock groan in pain. If things continued to go the same way, John Henry would surely lose.

The men began to get worried. Intimidated by the ferocious demeanor of the steam drill, they gradually backed their way out of the tunnel.

However, by midday, the sounds emitting from the tunnel had changed somewhat. The shrill and grating sounds of the steam drill continued as before, but they were no longer drowning out the ring of John Henry's hammers whose tones could be heard reverberating through the tunnel like the peeling bells resonating in some Buddhist temple...tinggg...tonggg...dinggg...donggg.

Then, in the space between the tones, John Henry's voice could be heard: "Drivin' steel is what I do"-Tinggg! Tonggg! I'm drivin' steel for my crew."-Dinggg! Donggg!

The men's faces brightened, and they began to chant the response, "John Henry!

John Henry! John Henry!"

The men's response thundering through the tunnel filled John Henry and renewed his strength and energy. The tempo of his strokes accelerated, their vibrating tones boring through the wall of rock.

The afternoon went quickly, and as the sun had begun its final descent, the tones of John Henry's hammers could still be heard, but his song was no longer in the air. So the men gathered on the other side of the mountain where the match would be decided. Their anxious stares were focused on the space of rock from which either the steam drill or John Henry would emerge.

As the setting sun poised itself on the horizon, its final rays beamed at the mountainside, a glint of steel caught the eyes of the onlooking crew. No one spoke. No one breathed. Then as the steel bit was forced through the wall of earth and rock, the unmistakable ring of John Henry's hammer could be heard. Within a matter of seconds John Henry hammered through the remaining shreds of rock and stepped into the dwindling rays of sunlight.

A joyous cheer erupted from the crew as they rushed forward to embrace John Henry. But before they could reach *him, he released his hammers and collapsed onto the bosom of his Mother Earth.*

He lay there quietly, allowing his waning smile to express his feelings of love for his companions. As the sun departed from the horizon, John Henry looked intently for the last time into the eyes of one of his crew, his voice the barest whisper.

"Will they understand what I did?" he asked.

And he was gone.

When Harlem Loved Me

It was back in the '40's.

Me 'n Ma,

Walkin' through the 'hood...

As we call it now.

I'd be holdin' her hand,

Sometimes...

'Cause I was real little then.

Other times,

I'd be runnin'up ahead.

It was such a warm, brown scene--

I mean warm with love.

The dark kinda spilled over

into the light,

And the light kinda spilled over

into the dark,

And it all came out brown to my infant eyes.

"Hey Ms. Ferguson!

That your little boy?

Looks just like you."

I felt so safe...

And loved.

It seemed like everybody knew Ma--

Bad little boys she had cared for

in nursery school.

Grown-ups of every description,

From black like my grandma

To pale gold like Ma.

And they all looked out for me

'Cause I was her child.

Yeah! I loved Harlem then,

And Harlem loved me.

Ali Rashid Abdullah

Man of the Moment

I used to see John Henry every day back then. His eight foot sandstone form guarded the archways that lead in and out of the courtyard of the housing project where I lived.

I used to see John Henry every day back then. His eight foot sandstone form guarded the archways that lead in and out of the courtyard of the housing project where I lived. In winter, his head was a target for our snowballs. I don't know what inspired John Louis Wilson, Jr., the Black architect who designed the Harlem River Houses, to choose John Henry as our guardian, but in light of current events, he couldn't have made a more fitting choice.

In this era of worldwide environmental concerns, the legend of John Henry focuses our attention on the primary characteristic of modern Western Civilization--the presence of modern technology as a dominating force in our lives. It is a tale that spotlights a period when America's transportation system was being expanded which, in turn would allow for the expansion of the techno-industrial system to the state as a whole. Today the realized expansion of that system has prompted cultural critic Neil Postman to coin the term "technopoly." The subtitle of his book of the same name, "The Surrender of Culture to Technology," aptly summarizes his conclusions.

What is so fascinating about the legend of John Henry is not only its ability to confront this situation well over 100 years ago, but also the character that is in the forefront of this confrontation. John Henry is an African American laborer, which in those days was as much akin to chattel slavery as the Jim Crow laws would allow. But the career choices for African Americans were rather limited, and most were lucky to have any kind of job.

And herein lies the irony of the situation, certainly as far as African Americans were concerned. On one hand the machine was regarded as a curse because it represented a threat to employees. But the "last hired, first fired" employment principle that was applied to African American employees made the machine an even greater threat to them. Then, on the other hand, the machine reduced the amount of human physical exertion required to accomplish a task. Since racist discrimination insured that African Americans would end up with the least desirable, most arduous tasks, machines were then simultaneously viewed as a blessing.

To illustrate, the cotton gin was an invention that combined the ingenious devices enslaved African Americans had created to ease the physiological damage done to their bodies due to the mass cultivation and harvesting of cotton. In another instance, the slave Joe Anderson was noted to have "assisted" Cyrus McCormick in his invention of the reaper. Then there was another slave, Henry Blair who invented a corn planter at approximately the same time as McCormick came out with the reaper. And, most notably, in relation to our current theme, "With a piece of gun barrel, some pewter, a couple of pieces of round steel, and some Materials," a slave named Benjamin Bradley, "constructed a *working model of a steam engine*." (W. L. Katz, Eyewitness, p. 119) And the list goes on.

The point is this: the devices being invented often ended up placing African Americans between the devil and the deep blue sea. On one hand, the machine reduced the most debilitating labor that was disproportionately doled out to them. But on the other, it undermined their already tenuous position in the work force.

When John Henry entered this picture the trend had already been set in motion. In fact, the recently ended Civil War was basically a conflict that arose from the implications of this trend. To be direct, the Industrial Revolution had begun in Europe, primarily in England. As the American colonies stabilized, the agricultural focus had become increasingly limited to the southern territories. Due to its topographical features and certain religious beliefs, the northern region came to focus more on industry. Initially as a colony and later on as a republic, overseas trade was destined to be a pillar of the American economy. Consequently, as the United States grew, it was inevitably drawn into competition with the mercantile nations of Europe. At the heart of this competition was the machine. More and more sophisticated machinery increased the speed of transportation and output in the manufacturing process. Those nations that lagged behind in technological growth got to foreign ports later and with fewer goods than their competitors.

Although sophisticated machinery was the latest factor in the quest for economic prosperity, the human being still remained essential. Someone had to be manufacturing, operating, and maintaining those machines, so a system had to be devised to facilitate this shift from an agricultural to an industrial economy. The expansion of wage labor, termed "wage slavery" by some, became the bedrock of the new order. Without this human energy as a given, the economic principles contained in the bible of industrial nations, Adam Smith's, Wealth of Nations, would be unfeasible.

In fact, the much-misunderstood axiom about machinery is that it increases labor rather than diminishes it as the myth implies. True enough, in the initial stages individuals may be displaced. And, true enough, there may be a reduction in the labor required to harvest a crop of vegetables, for instance. However, in order to save labor on one end, it must be increased on the other. That is to say, the manufacturing of new machinery requires an increase in mining, the development of new plants to process the metals, the development of new factories to manufacture the machines, the development of a management sector to organize and supervise labor, the development of an office sector to deal with related paperwork, the development of a maintenance sector to maintain and repair the machinery, and, in many cases, the development of an educational sector to train employees in the use of new machinery. These are some areas that immediately come to mind. You can probably think of others. But the bottom line is that machines do not reduce labor, they increase it. Of course

America's racist policies would insure that African Americans would be the last chosen for these new employment opportunities.

But from the American South's perspective, they didn't need "labor-saving" machinery. They had an abundance of human beings who functioned like machines and were self propagating. So their philosophy was "If it ain't broke, don't fix it."

But the North had seen the economic handwriting on the wall. If the United States were to continue to compete in the international arena, the entire nation would have to shift its priorities from agriculture to industry. Otherwise Europe would leave them far behind.

Slavery didn't become an issue because the North had suddenly realized that slavery was immoral. Slavery, then, became an issue in the civil conflict because its eradication would undermine the economic foundations of the South enabling the North to gain the upper hand. Furthermore, in the industrial system, chattel slavery, as a basis of one's economic structure, was not perceived as a prudent way to proceed. So it becomes clear that the Civil War was not fought to end racial injustice. If there were any doubts in anyone's mind, the Northern betrayal of the African American following Reconstruction should have made the North's position crystal clear.

Which is not to say that no European Americans ever opposed slavery and racial injustice. To their credit, many did. And they deserve to be applauded. However, despite their often ardent efforts, they have never been able to convince the majority to take action to put an end to racial injustice and abuse.

It is within this social climate, then, that John Henry takes action. On the surface, it may seem strange that an African American would bother. One might think that the lesson of Crispus Attuck's martyrdom in the American Revolution should have been learned. Remember, after the European Americans defeated the Europeans with the help of African Americans, American slavery became more repressive than ever. As was to be the case after the Civil War as well, armed service would not gain African Americans social justice in the United States.

Yet, here was another African American, John Henry, seemingly getting in the middle of a fight between two groups of white folks. On one side, there was the South, seething with resentment from its defeat in the Civil War and having to be dragged kicking and screaming into the Industrial Age. On the other, there was the North, all aglow with its victory and bubbling over with pride and enthusiasm each time a new "time-saving," "labor-saving," power-gaining device was conceived.

But John Henry raised a concern that had seemingly been forgotten somewhere along the way. It was the issue of human worth and dignity. As he put it, "A man is more than a machine," and he set out to prove it. In the end, John Henry would resurrect the spirit of Crispus Attucks in his one-man revolution against the tyranny of the machine in our lives. The symbolism of his act was so profound that he became a legendary figure, not only among African Americans but also eventually among all Americans. The legend of John Henry touched a chord that continues to resonate within the souls of all Americans and, quite possibly, all human beings. This was no mean feat for an African American in a society where race has been made into a dividing line. For some reason though, *everyone* identifies with John Henry, pulls for him to win, applauds his victory, and mourns his death.

There are some who perceive John Henry's death as a sign of the ultimate power and victory of modern technology. They perceive its power to be indomitable, its march to be inevitable, and its effects to be irreproachable. But death is unavoidable. It comes to all creatures. With such an eventuality in mind, the question is will we have demonstrated our worth when death comes.

Or, as Rev., Dr. Martin Luther King, Jr. reminds us, if "one day some great opportunity stands before you, and calls for you to stand up for some great principle, some great issue, some great cause…" "… you must do it because it has gripped you so much that you are willing to die for it if necessary." "I say to you this morning that if you have never found something so dear and so precious to you that you will die for it, then you aren't fit to live." John Henry's demonstration of his worth earned him legendary status, not only among his peers, but also in the hearts and minds of future generations. When John Henry challenged the steam drill, he simultaneously challenged the ideas that had initiated and sustained its existence. In effect, John Henry had chosen to become dead to those short-sighted ideas that lie at the root of today's world-wide social disharmony and environmental destruction. In the final analysis, time bears witness that death neither finished John Henry nor his work. He has been resurrected to live on as a legend, and both human rights and environmental activists throughout the world carry on his work.

Perhaps the reason this incident (regardless of the degree of factual evidence) was able to capture the imagination of so many and become a legend is because the human soul glimpsed the Truth contained therein and grasped onto it when it appeared in the legend of John Henry. Now, over one hundred years hence, we are better able to see the folly of the Industrial *Revolution*. We can now see that "progress" is a relative term depending upon one's destination. Only if environmental ruin and social disharmony were the intended destination of Western civilization could Westerners say that progress has been achieved. It is now apparent that the term "revolution" has no bearing whatsoever on the consumption, pollution, and destruction that accompanies modern technological "development."

We can see now that real revolution is a cycle. As Russell Means, the American Indian activist put it, "Mother Earth will retaliate, the whole environment will retaliate, and the abusers will be eliminated. Things come full circle, back to where they started. That's revolution."

John Henry intuitively sensed the impending crisis. As a "natural man"--a man in synch with his nature as a human being--he knew his worth. But humanity seemed in danger of forgetting their worth. Therefore a symbolic act was called for--an act that has become an immortal statement to humankind. His victory over the steam drill immediately earned John Henry a place in the hearts of his fellow human beings and has insured his immortality in their minds.

Interestingly enough, at one time Paul Bunyan was a legendary American hero whose status was at least equal to John Henry's. However, at the opening of the twenty-first century, in the era of "global warming," "the greenhouse effect," "ozone depletion," and "destruction of the Amazonian rain forests and North American redwood groves," Paul Bunyan's now questionable work as a logger is steadily diminishing his popularity. By contrast, John Henry seemed to be in synch with the pulse of the future. He is remembered for having defended the worth of human beings above machines. Consequently John Henry remains a beacon of light to guide those who choose to work toward living in *harmony* within themselves, with other human beings, and with their environment.

John Henry's Vision

The thought wouldn't leave John Henry's mind. He didn't care at first. In fact, he kind of savored the idea–"A man is **more** than a machine!" When it initially entered his mind, it had propelled him into action. "I can beat that machine," he had declared.

But now he needed some rest. The match was scheduled to begin at daybreak, but the thought kept reverberating in his mind–"A man is **more** than a machine!" It wouldn't go away.

John Henry lay stretched out on his back looking up at the poles that intersected to form the roof of his tent. The earth beneath his ground tarp was warm and yielded to his bulky frame. He hadn't slept in a bed since before he left home. John Henry had outgrown beds long ago. Anyway, those cots that were issued at campsites to the railroad workers were barely big enough to support one of John Henry's legs.

He drew his massive arms from beneath the two blankets that were sewn together lengthwise to serve as his cover. Then he clasped his hands behind the back of his head just above his neck. His elbows stuck out like the wings of some huge airborne creature from primordial times.

Although it was after midnight, light from the full moon entered his tent through the flap at the top. He usually kept the flap open when weather permitted. The moonlight illuminated everything in the tent, and from the corner of his eye John Henry could see the form of his two hammers standing like two sentries. They stood one on each side of his head, guarding him as he slept. Those hammers had been with John Henry for so long it seemed as though they were a part of his body. In fact, he had been known to say that when he put his hammers down, he felt he had taken off part of his arms.

"Ahhh!"

John Henry suddenly uttered a sound of quiet understanding to no one in particular–or so it seemed. Then, just as suddenly, the involuntary mantra that had been intruding upon his sleep halted. It was John Henry's hammers. The words recurring in his head–"A man is **more** than a machine!"–had been emanating from his hammers.

John Henry sat up and spun around so he could see both hammers at once. The rich oak arms of the handles glistened *from the oil that had seeped into them from John Henry's calloused hands. The branching veins of wood grain made their way down the shafts to unflinching black fists of hardened steel that sat, knuckles down, on the blue tarp. Grown men swore they had seen railroad spikes sink into the ground in terror when John Henry swung his hammers.*

The silence seemed to deepen in John Henry's tent. It was the respectful silence of anticipation an audience gives an artist just prior to his performance. John Henry arose slowly, until he stood like a giant sequoia, his head inches away from the roof of the tent. He then bent forward, wrapping a powerful hand around each gleaming oak shaft.

The hammers, quivering with expectancy, seemed to jump into John Henry's hands. Their vibration went through his arms like an electric shock and coursed through his chest terminating at his heart. Once there, the words of the mantra—"A man is **more** than a machine!"—seemed to press and knead John Henry's heart like the hands of a skillful masseur. As his heart's rhythm adjusted to the refrain, the words began to stream through his veins, entering every cell in his body.

John Henry needed more space. He strode out into the moonlight still grasping his hammers. (No, "grasping" is not the word. Actually, John Henry required no more of an exertion of force to hold his hammers than he did to keep his hands connected to his wrists.) He kept walking until he came to the site of last night's campfire where he had challenged the Northerner and his steam drill machine.

The fire had diminished leaving a bed of glowing timbers that would be a mound of gray ash in the morning. Standing at the edge of the circle of boulders that had contained the fire, John Henry sunk the head of each hammer into the surface of red-hot embers. Immediately the heat began to course through his body, warming him against the night's chill.

Just before the wooden shafts burst into flame, John Henry withdrew the heads from the embers—each one now a luminous tempered brick. Slowly he began to alternately swing his hammers over his head.

Faster and faster his arms moved until there appeared two red circular figures that traced the path his hammers took as they traveled through space on each side of John Henry.

Faster and faster his arms moved until there appeared two red circular figures that traced the path his hammers took as they traveled through space on each side of John Henry. Gradually John Henry's body began to rise up off the ground. In a matter of seconds he had risen several hundred yards above the campsite. As he looked down, he could see his campmates emerging from their tents. The sound of howling wind created by John Henry revolving his hammers had awakened them, and they immediately feared a hurricane or tornado was about to rip through their camp and that they, along with their campsite, would be demolished. But, as John Henry had gained in altitude, the wind had diminished, so the men felt greatly relieved.

As they were heading back to their tents, one cautious soul decided to check the night sky one final time for signs of any remaining turbulence. Glowing in the darkness just above the peak that capped Big Bend Tunnel, he spotted what looked like a pair of fiery crimson rings.

"Hey!" he exclaimed to his companions. "Would ya looka there!"

The rings were becoming dimmer and dimmer, however; and by the time the other men looked to where he was pointing, they had disappeared from sight.

The man rubbed his eyes and looked again, but there was no evidence of anything to be found. His partners were too *weary from the prior day's work to even tease him. They just shook their heads and silently trudged back to their tents.*

Meanwhile, John Henry had returned to Earth right on top of the peak over Big Bend Tunnel. As he had slowed the speed of his arms' revolutions, his body had gradually descended to the ground. He was atop the very mountain through which his match with the steam drill would take place. In his descent, the red glow in the heads of his hammers had diminished bit by bit, and they now had the appearance of two gleaming bricks of obsidian.

*John Henry felt the urge to release his hammers, and he left them standing one on each side of him. But their mantra—"A man is **more** than a machine!"—continued to resonate within* *his being with each beat of his heart. However, the refrain, like his heartbeat, no longer distracted him. It had merged with his being, bringing a new clarity and purpose to his life.*

John Henry sat cross-legged on the ground between his hammers. The need for rest had been replaced with a potent, but controlled, influx of energy that lightly flowed into his body with every breath. He bent forward and placed his hands, palms down, on the earth in front of him, feeling the pulse of the planet.

As he sat touching the earth, John Henry became overwhelmed with sadness. Tears filled his eyes and began flowing down his cheeks to the earth beneath him. John Henry could feel the pain, which his Mother Earth was anticipating. He felt the gouging wounds that would be thoughtlessly inflicted upon her when men became even more consumed with greed

for the treasures that were stored within her bosom. He felt

how difficult it would be for her to breathe when men covered

her body with innumerable roads of concrete and tar, deposited

unprecedented forms and amounts of waste beneath her skin,

injected her veins and arteries with the poisonous residues from

their reckless experiments, and filled her atmosphere with the

smoke and fumes of indescribably noxious gases. He heard

the strident shrieks, squeals, screams, wails, and whistles; the

raucous grinding, clanking, grating, rasping, and scraping; the

grieved moaning, howling, whining, and groaning of the Earth's

metals as they were forced to submit to incredible pressures,

temperatures, and speeds.

The water from John Henry's eyes continued to flow, now forming a steady stream down the side of the mountain. Unable to bear the pain any longer, John Henry looked to the heavens for respite. In desperation, he stretched his arms toward the stars, his hands and fingers extended to their fullest.

"I see! My Lord God, I see!" John Henry's plaintive cry echoed his sorrow through the heavens.

*Indeed, John Henry did see. He painstakingly returned his hands to the Earth, once again feeling the steady throb of her pulse. The pain had subsided, and in its place John Henry felt an irresistible rhythm that touched him in the depths of his soul. It was **his** rhythm, the rhythm of **his heart**, pumping through the Earth...or was it the Earth's rhythm, pumping through John*

Henry? It didn't matter. What did matter was that by touching the Earth, John Henry was able to feel his synchronicity with the pulse of creation.

The message was finally fully clear. When John Henry swung his hammers, his body's movement was a dance in space, his hammer's ring was music for the universe, and the Earth vibrated to her child's living presence, for John Henry was created from the clay of the Earth. His hammers allowed John Henry to touch the Earth with his own unique rhythms, which were alive in his work. It was his energy, his coordination, his power—in a word, it was his "nature" that was not rendered obsolete. But the machine would rob humankind of this opportunity. If unopposed, it would render the "natural man" extinct.

John Henry would have none of it. In fact, he now realized that the railroad was the system that would deliver the implements that would gradually wreak havoc upon all of creation. He rose to his feet and began to walk down the mountainside in a direction away from the campsite. He had only gone about twenty yards when the mantra began to impose itself upon his consciousness again—"A man is **more** than a machine!" Yes, he knew that—now more clearly than ever. That was why he was walking away.

He started to walk again, feeling a great sense of loss. He turned and saw his hammers standing side-by-side on the crest of the mountain. It was then that he realized he was turning his back on his destiny. With renewed conviction, John Henry *reversed his direction, retrieved his hammers, and began his descent toward the campsite. He knew what he must do. His action would be a declaration of his consciousness to the world. What more can any mortal do? Then he would be done with it.*

The men awoke the next morning to find a stream flowing right through the middle of the camp. They looked toward the opening in the mountainside where the match would take place, and there stood John Henry, big and baaad as ever, with a hammer in each hand.

About the Author:

Author Ali Rashid Abdullah's latest work takes us to a crossroad in the evolution of modern society. He suggests we return to the legend of John Henry for direction in a world that has become dominated by the theories of science and the gadgetry of technology.

In his work Challenging Technopoly: The Vision of John Henry, Abdullah combines a number of literary elements reminiscent of the manner employed in Harlem Renaissance writer Jean Toomer's classic novel Cane. He tells two stories. The first is a re-telling of the original Legend of John Henry. The second is an original piece entitled John Henry's Vision that seeks to reveal the vision latent in the classic legend. Abdullah also presents an essay that examines the basis for John Henry's oppositional stance against the technological wizardry of his era. Another literary element included is a poignant poem that re-creates the Harlem setting of Abdullah's childhood where he first encountered the figure of John Henry.

As in the original "Legend," there is a challenge being put forth here in Abdullah's work -- a challenge that questions the notion of science and technology being our primary source of wisdom and our irrefutable voice of authority. Indeed, rather than discarding John Henry's ideas as "old-fashioned," Abdullah perceives them to be right on time.

Printed in the United States
By Bookmasters